If I Swam With Jonah

By Pamela Moritz

Illustrated by MacKenzie Haley

APPLES & HONEY PRESS

To Mom, for her giant-size love,
and to her other little fish, EJ and Joe

–PM

To my loving, supportive parents

–MH

The illustrations in this book were created with mixed media and digital painting.

Apples & Honey Press
An Imprint of Behrman House Publishers
Millburn, New Jersey 07041
www.applesandhoneypress.com

Library of Congress Cataloging-in-Publication Data

Names: Moritz, Pamela, 1965- author. | Haley, MacKenzie, illustrator.
Title: If I swam with Jonah / by Pamela Moritz ; illustrated by MacKenzie Haley.
Description: Millburn, New Jersey : Apples and Honey Press, [2022] |
Audience: Grades K-1. | Summary: "A young boy imagines that he has an
adventure with the biblical Jonah"-- Provided by publisher.
Identifiers: LCCN 2020055945 | ISBN 9781681155739 (hardcover)
Subjects: LCSH: Jonah (Biblical prophet)--Juvenile fiction. | CYAC: Stories
in rhyme. | Jonah (Biblical prophet) | Imagination--Fiction.
Classification: LCC PZ8.3.M8138 Ii 2022 | DDC [E]--dc23
LC record available at https://lccn.loc.gov/2020055945

Design by Rina Schachter
Edited by Ann D. Koffsky & Aviva Gutnick
Printed in China

1 3 5 7 9 8 6 4 2

You're the best little fish, and I love little you, but imagine-a fish, **_giant-sized_**!

She could swallow up Jonah and bring me along. Can you picture it? Just close your eyes.

If I saw a big fish, twice the size of a ship,
and she swam by my boat in the sea,

if that fish opened wide showing Jonah inside,
I would holler, "Hey, fish, wait for me!"

Oh, how great! She would wait!
"But he's **grouchy**," she'd warn.

A time-out? In a *fish*?!
Jonah needed a friend!
I would slippity slide in and find him.

"Thanks for coming," he'd frown,
"but I'm hungry and wet."
"Well, we *are* in the sea," I'd remind him.

I would hand him a towel and search in my bag.
"If you're hungry," I'd say, "I can help."
Then I'd pull out my bread and make sandwiches,
gathering seaweed and seagrass and kelp.

"That's delicious!" he'd say.
"And I'm glad that you've joined me.
It's lonely alone in this belly."
He'd lean in and whisper, "It's also *so* boring,
and . . . don't tell the fish, but she's ***smelly***."

"I can hear you!" the fish would reply, laughing loudly.
Her belly, like Jell-O, would jiggle.

Poor Jonah might tumble and cry, "It's an earthquake!"
"A **fishquake**!" I'd say, and he'd giggle.

She'd proclaim, "What a notion! I smell like the ocean.
You might want to see what lies in it.

It's loaded with colorful creatures in motion—
I'll let you swim out for a minute."

I'd lunge for my gear, handing over some goggles.
"Take these," I'd say. "Please, they're for you."

We'd splash and we'd swim, maybe somersault in.
What a world! What an undersea **ZOO**!

Maybe then I would notice a dolphin was caught
in the ropes of a fisherman's net!

I'd twist, pull, and pry 'til the ropes were untied.
"You can go, dolphin, sir. You're all set."

Instead he would give us a somersault show.
We'd "**Woo-hoo!**" and yell, "This is the best!"

We'd return when the fish said,
"Let's go for a dive!

The deep is a great place to rest."

But what if that dive made it darker and darker,
and Jonah sat shaking, eyes tight?

I'd pull out my flashlight and say, "Don't be frightened."
I'd flick it on, "Let there be light!"

"Hmm, you know something?" Jonah would quietly tell me.
"The fish . . .
            and the dolphin . . .
                        and you . . .

You seem happy to help and to share—like you *like* it."
I'd laugh and say,

*"Jonah,
we do!"*

"Well, I'm ready to try it," he'd say standing up.
And he'd cup both his hands and he'd shout,

"Those people in Nineveh need my help *now*.
Dear fish, can you please ***let me out***?"

"So you're ready? I'm proud!" fish would holler out loud.
"Then there's no need for little ol' me!"

She'd surface, then—
ptooey!
We'd land in the sand.

"It was fun, but you're done. You're both free!"

"Even though you might smell, you're a great fish hotel!"
I would yell. "Fish, I wish I could kiss you!"

With a wink and a wave, she'd dive right out of sight,
and I'd hear Jonah whisper, "I'll miss you."

Then he'd stand and he'd hand me a gift made of shells.
"Don't forget how you helped me at sea.

When you followed that fish twice the size of a ship, kid,
it made all the difference to **me**!"

A NOTE FOR FAMILIES

Have you ever been told to do something that you didn't want to do? In the Bible's telling of *Jonah*, that's just what happens: God tells Jonah to help the people of Nineveh by bringing them an important message, but Jonah doesn't want to. Instead, he runs away and boards a ship. Then he gets tossed overboard and swallowed by a giant fish. He's stuck inside it for three whole days!

That must have been enough time for him to think about how important it is to help others, because Jonah finally decides to go to Nineveh and help the people there by sharing God's message with them.

Whenever I've read the Bible story, it's made me wonder: What did Jonah *do* during those three days? What happened in that time that made him realize the importance of helping others? Those questions inspired me to write *If I Swam with Jonah,* where I imagined the answers: Jonah spent those three days with a young friend who showed him how good it feels to help.

What questions do you have about the story of Jonah? What does it make *you* wonder?

Shalom,

Pam